Dick Bruna

CHAS

SIMON AND SCHUSTER

It happened one dark night, long, long ago.

There were shepherds in the field, keeping watch over their sheep.

They were talking to each other, when suddenly they saw a light.

The light was so bright and so beautiful that day seemed to be dawning.

But that was not so.

The light came from an angel,

an angel with a message sent by God.

Do not be afraid, said the angel, for the shepherds

really were a little frightened.

I come to tell you something wonderful, just listen.

In Bethlehem a child is born, whose name is Jesus

and who will bring joy to all people.

Go now and see him, wrapped in linen cloths and lying in a manger.

When the angel had spoken, there came another angel,
and after that another and another, until the sky
was filled with angels.
And all the angels sang a song together.
So sweet was the sound of their song that sheep and shepherds
stood still in the field to listen.
Glory be to God, they sang, glory be to God on high
and peace on earth.

When the song had ended, the angels disappeared.

Oh, how beautiful that was, said the shepherds, turning to each other.

Let us go at once to Bethlehem, then we can see

what the angel told us.

And they set out.

After they had been walking quite a while, they came to a stable.
It was a white stable, with green wooden doors
and a window that could not be closed because there was no shutter.
It was a stable where the animals could sleep
when it was too cold outside.

Can it be here? the shepherds asked each other.

Could Jesus be born in a stable?

The angel had said that they would find him

wrapped in cloths and lying in a manger.

And a manger is a trough from which the cattle feed.

Come on, let's go inside, the shepherds said.

And they found a baby who was wrapped in cloths
and lying in a manger, just as the angel said.
Mary and Joseph stood beside the manger.
The shepherd moved quietly towards them.
Oh, how happy they were to have discovered Jesus.
And they told Mary and Joseph about the message
the angel had brought to them.

Do you know who else was going to the stable in Bethlehem?

Three wise kings.

One with a white beard, one with a black

and one without a beard, but with a black and kindly face.

They wore fine robes of yellow, red and green,

and gold crowns on their heads.

And they rode on camels.

When they arrived at last, they climbed
down from their camels, and all three brought out
a precious gift.
The king with the white beard brought out a splendid cup
of frankincense.
The king with the black beard, a little box of gold.
And the king with the black face a cup of myrrh.

When the kings came to the stable, Mary took the child
out of the manger so that they could see him well.
They gave their frankincense and myrrh and gold to him.
It was for him that they had brought them there.
How glad the kings were to have found the child,
he who had come to bring happiness to everyone.
When Mary asked them how they knew Jesus was born
here in this stable, the black-bearded king
told her this story. Listen now.

One evening the three kings, who lived in distant lands,

had seen a star so beautiful that they had met together,

for they said:

a very special child must have been born

when such a glorious star appeared in heaven.

Let us go now and find him, and take him noble gifts.

And they had climbed on their camels

and the star had pointed out the way.

When he had told his tale, the king with the white beard said: Now let us go, we have to make a long, long journey home. Quietly they went away, and Mary stood with Joseph, waving until they were out of sight.